Other Lothrop, Lee & Shepard Books
by Jan Ormerod
*Sunshine, Moonlight, Rhymes Around the Day,
101 Things to Do with a Baby*

For Lynne

Library of Congress Cataloging in Publication Data
Ormerod, Jan.
Reading.
(Jan Ormerod's Baby books)
Summary: Baby plays over, under, and around Dad while he is reading.
1. Children's stories, English. [1. Babies—Fiction. 2. Fathers—Fiction]
I. Title.   II. Series: Ormerod, Jan. Baby books.
PZ7. 0634Re   1985   [E]   84-12628
ISBN 0-688-04127-2

Reading

Jan Ormerod

LOTHROP, LEE & SHEPARD BOOKS

NEW YORK

Climbing over,

crawling under,

looking through,

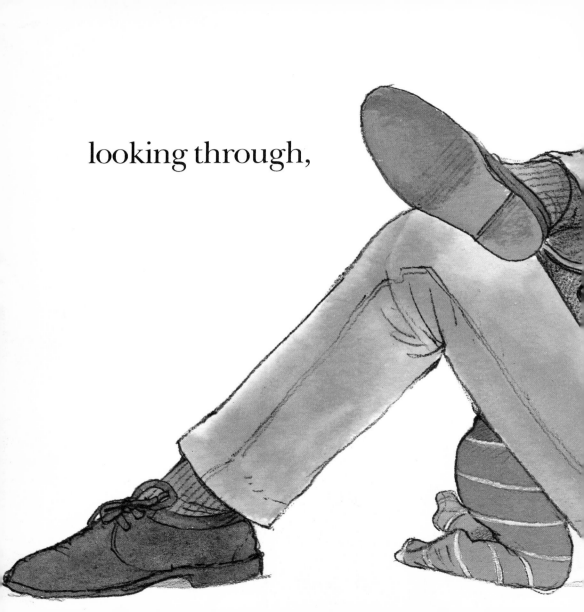

pushing through,
climbing up,

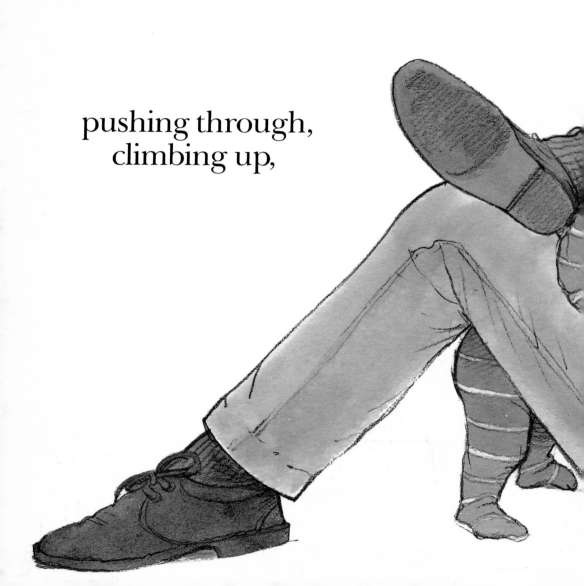

relaxing,

peeping over,

reading.